This Oscar book belongs to:

....

....

D0537539

70003127341X

For Mum and Dad
G.W.

The author and publisher would like
to thank Sue Ellis at the Centre for Literacy in
Primary Education, Martin Jenkins and Paul Harrison
for their invaluable input and guidance
during the making of this book.

First published 2006 by Walker Books Ltd
87 Vauxhall Walk, London SE11 5HJ

This edition published 2007

10 9 8 7 6 5 4 3 2 1

© 2006 Geoff Waring

The right of Geoff Waring to be identified as author-illustrator
of this work has been asserted by him in accordance with the
Copyright, Designs and Patents Act 1988

This book has been typeset in ITCKabel

Printed in China

British Library Cataloguing in Publication Data:
a catalogue record for this book is available from the British Library

IISBN 978-1-4063-0498-5

www.walkerbooks.co.uk

WALKER BOOKS
AND SUBSIDIARIES
LONDON · BOSTON · SYDNEY · AUCKLAND

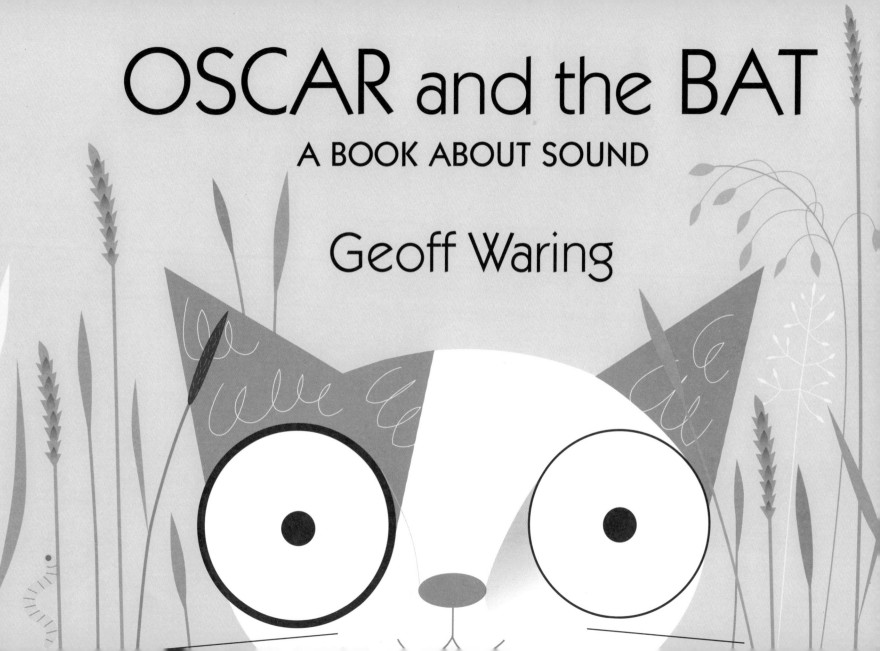

OSCAR and the BAT

A BOOK ABOUT SOUND

Geoff Waring

One summer evening, in the meadow, Oscar heard a new sound. He looked around to see who was making it.

Bat swooped by.

"It's the baby blackbirds," he said. "Their nest is over there in the bush."

"Oh," said Oscar. "So I can hear them, even though I can't see them."

"Yes," said Bat. "Our ears help us know what's around us, even when our eyes don't."

Cheep. cheep. cheep. cheep. cheep

♪ Sreeeeee-sree-tweee ♪

Then Oscar heard another sound.
This time he could see who was making it.

"The blackbird's singing to warn other blackbirds
to stay away from his nest," Bat said.

Oscar thought it was the loveliest sound
he had ever heard.

"I wish I could sing like a blackbird!" he said.

"Kittens can make other sounds," Bat said. "So can bats!"

Squeak

Miaow

"We make sounds in our throats," Bat went on, "but some animals talk with different parts of their bodies."

Many male grasshoppers talk to female grasshoppers by rubbing their wings together.

Chirruh chirp

Some cockroaches make sounds to one another through holes along their sides.

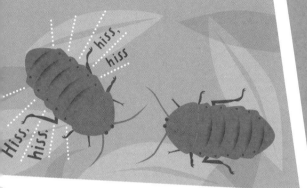

Hiss. hiss. hiss. hiss

When they nest, some male hummingbirds make a loud sound with their wings to warn other birds away.

Whistle.

whirrrr

Rattle. rattle

Click. whistle. squeak

Bottlenose dolphins send messages to each other underwater through their blowholes.

The tips of rattlesnakes' tails have hard connecting ridges. If other animals come too close, they lift and shake their tails as a warning.

"Are all sounds 'talking sounds'?" Oscar asked.

"Lots are," Bat said, "but nearly everything makes a sound when it moves. Close your eyes and listen. What can you hear moving in the meadow?"

Grass makes no sound when it's still, but swishes when the wind moves it.

Swish

Swish

Swish

Swish

Swish

Swish

Brroooom

Machines are still and silent
until they are switched on.
Then their engines move
and make noises.

Still water in a pond is silent,
but moving water makes sounds.

Gurgle,
gurgle

Gurgle, gurgle

Gurgle,
gurgle

Rumble, rumble

Rumble, rumble

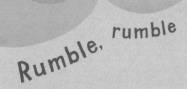

Oscar could hear another sound. It was in the sky.
"What's that rumbling?" he asked.

"Thunder," said Bat. "There's a storm coming.
Even though it's far away, we can still hear
the thunder because it's such a big sound."

Rumble, rumble   Rumble, rumble   Rumble, rumble

Oscar opened his eyes. "It's getting louder!" he said.

"The thunder's coming this way," Bat said.
"The closer it is to us, the louder it sounds to us…

Rumble, CRA

"And when a big noise is very near …

SH!

it sounds very loud indeed!"
Bat shouted, as Oscar leapt away.

Safe under the leaves, Oscar listened to raindrops falling. "The rain is very near too," he said, "but it isn't scary."

Pitter. patter

Pitter. patter

Pitter. patter

18

Pitter. patter

Pitter. patter

patter

"The rain is making a
soft sound," Bat said,
"not a harsh sound
like the thunder."

When the rain stopped, Oscar put out his head to listen. "Is the thunder going away now?" he asked.

"Yes," said Bat. "The further away it is from us, the quieter it sounds to us."

Rumble, rumble   Rumble, rumble

Then it was gone.

"I can't hear anything," Oscar whispered.

"No," whispered Bat. "This is silence –
or it would be, if we weren't whispering!"

But just then…

21

"The cow sounds a bit like the thunder!" said Oscar.

"Yes," said Bat. "Cows make a deep sound.
It's low and rumbly. It isn't high and squeaky,
like the sound the baby birds made."

Now the blackbird started to sing again.

"That's still my favourite sound," said Oscar.
"It keeps changing. And it's never too loud
and scary, or too high and squeaky.
It's just right, like music!"

And he started to purr...

Purrrrrrrrrrr

"And *that's* my favourite sound," said Oscar's mother, who had come to fetch him.

But Oscar and Bat were listening so hard, they didn't even notice her.

Thinking some more about sound

Listening

Our ears help us to know what's happening around us.

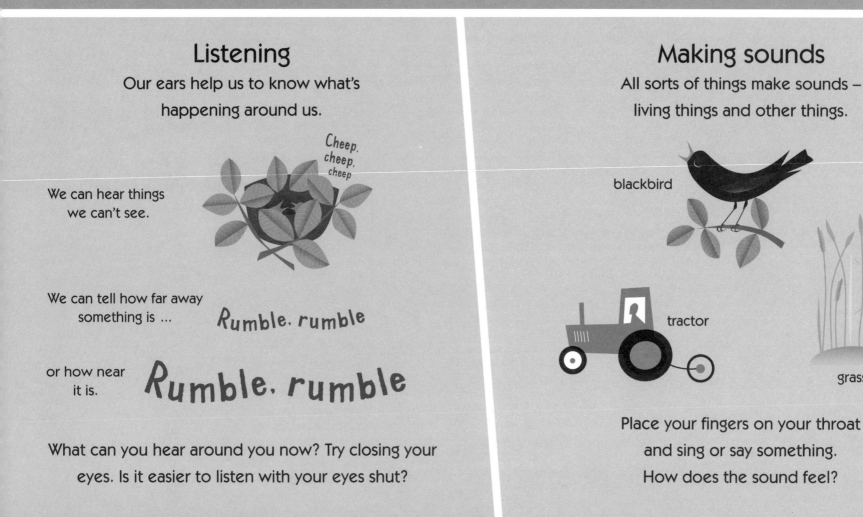

Cheep, cheep, cheep

We can hear things we can't see.

We can tell how far away something is ...

Rumble, rumble

or how near it is.

Rumble, rumble

What can you hear around you now? Try closing your eyes. Is it easier to listen with your eyes shut?

Making sounds

All sorts of things make sounds – living things and other things.

blackbird

tractor

grass

Place your fingers on your throat and sing or say something. How does the sound feel?

Different sounds

There are many kinds of sound. Some opposites help us to think about their differences.

Moooooo!

deep

Cheep, cheep

high

Rumble, rumble

harsh

Pitter, patter

soft

♪ *Chirrrr-churra-chirrup* ♪

lovely

CRASH!

scary

What are your favourite sounds?

Index

Oscar thinks sound is great! Do you too?

OSCAR and the FROG
A BOOK ABOUT GROWING
Geoff Waring

OSCAR and the MOTH
A BOOK ABOUT LIGHT AND DARK
Geoff Waring

OSCAR and the BAT
A BOOK ABOUT SOUND
Geoff Waring

OSCAR and the CRICKET
A BOOK ABOUT MOVING AND ROLLING
Geoff Waring

Which of these Oscar books have you read?